His Best Friend
A Psychotic Thriller

His Best Friend
A Psychotic Thriller

BY

TRACY WILSON

http://beautifulpublications.com

Published by
Beautiful Publications LLC
Stratford, CT 06614

PRINT ISBN: 978-1-7356620-5-3
EBOOK ISBN: 978-1-7356620-4-6

Printed in the United States of America

Introduction

My name is Clarisse. I met Randall a few months ago when I started going to R & R Gym – (Randall & Rashad). I thought R & R was about Rest & Rejuvenation until Rashad approached me. He was nice and professional – but he was a grimy mutha fucka. You're probably wondering how I came to this conclusion after I just said he was nice and professional – I felt it. That man made my skin crawl the moment he touched me – and his eyes confirmed it. Thank God Randall came over to rescue me or I would've run out of there and never looked back.

Chapter 1

"So Clarisse – are you ready to get started on your fitness journey?" Rashad asked...

"Well... I thought I was..." I hesitated...

"Hey Rashad..." the young lady greeted as she came in...

"Hey Angela..." he greeted... "Excuse me – that's my regular appointment – if you decide you want to sign up, let me know..." he said as he hurried after Angela...

"Oh thank God..." I mumbled under my breath as I got up to leave...

"Are you leaving?" the gentleman asked as he hurried over to me...

"Yes..."

"May I ask why?"

"Who are you?" I asked as I turned around and looked him in his face. I tried to be indignant but when he smiled at me I softened instantly...

"I'm Randall..." he answered. I wanted to kiss his lips as soon as he opened his mouth...

"Stop it Clarisse – remember what happened with Darryl!" I thought, chastising myself...

"And you are?" he asked as he took my hand, snapping me out of my trance...

"Huh?"

"Pleased to meet you Huh..." he said and then we both bust out laughing...

"I'm sorry..." I laughed... "My name is Clarisse..."

"Nice to meet you Clarisse..." he laughed... "Come with me to my office..." he said as he took my hand and led me to his office. When we got to his office, he opened the door for me, I went in, he came in, and when he closed the door I got nervous... "I can open the door if that will make you more comfortable..."

"Thank you – I appreciate that..." I said as he opened the door and went behind his desk to sit down...

"Please – have a seat..." I sat down in front of him and he continued... "So what brought you in today?"

"Well... I like to work out..."

"Okay – what brought you in here?"

"I don't understand..."

"What made you pick this gym?"

"Oh – now I understand – I picked this gym because you're small..."

"I'm glad to hear you say that..."

"Really?"

"Oh yea – we've lost clients because they thought we're too small..."

"That doesn't make any sense – you can only use one piece of equipment at a time!" I laughed...

"I agree – but I don't mind – we have plenty of clients – and because we're a small gym we're able to cater to our clients that choose to stay..."

"That's what I'm looking for..."

"Does that mean you've changed your mind about us?" he asked as he smiled at me again...

"Stop it Clarisse!" I scolded to myself...

"Clarisse?"

"Oh – yes – I've changed my mind..."

"Good – now are you looking for a place to come work out a few times a week or do you need a personal trainer?"

"What do you think?" I answered as I stood up and put my hands on my hips...

"I think you're beautiful..." he answered as he smiled at me again...

"Thank you – but that's not what I meant..." I laughed...

"What did you mean then?" he asked as he smiled at me again. I started to think he knew what he was doing so I smiled back at him as I answered his question with a question...

"Do I need a personal trainer?"

"Have you ever had a personal trainer?"

"No..."

"Then the answer is yes..."

"Why? I'm not new to working out..."

"I can see that..." he said as he smiled at me again. At this point I knew he knew what he was doing and I decided to stop caring. So what he was smiling at me? So what he finds me attractive – what's wrong with that?

"So why do I need a personal trainer then?"

"As your personal trainer, my job is to make sure your workout benefits your body and helps you reach your maximum potential..." he answered as he got up from behind the desk and came towards me... "Do you mind?" he asked as he put his hands on my waist...

"I don't mind..." I didn't mind at all...

"You see these muscles here?" he asked as he ran his hand up my right side up to below my breast...

"I didn't realize I had any muscles there..." I laughed...

"You do – most of us concentrate on the mid-section, but I can tell you concentrate on your waist as well..." he said as he moved his hand back down to my waist...

"So does that mean I've been working towards my maximum potential?" I asked as I smiled first this time...

"Absolutely..."

"So what can you do for me?"

"Well..." he said as he let go of my waist and stepped back... "I can tell you're not a beginner – which is good – this means I can get you into a regular routine that will work for you and we can target any areas you feel you want to target..." he answered as he went to sit back down...

"Okay..."

"The gym membership is $19 per month – this gives you unlimited access to classes, the machines, the showers – and on Wednesday you can bring a guest with you – if your guest decides to sign up with us, you'll get an hour of my time for free..."

"What if I want a personal trainer along with my membership?"

"My normal rate is $60 per hour – but as a member of the gym that rate goes from $60 per hour to $39 per hour..."

"How does that work?"

"You sign up for a monthly membership of $19 per month – anytime you want to see me, you schedule an appointment with me, you pay me separately, we meet here, and you work out with me..."

"Okay – I'll start by signing up for the gym membership..."

"Thank you – just fill out this application and I'll get you set up..." he said as he smiled at me again...

"Can I ask you a personal question?"

"Sure..."

"Are you married?"

"Why?"

"I wanted to make sure I didn't have to worry about your wife running up on me..." I laughed...

"You would never have to worry about that – my girlfriend broke up with me for something that had nothing to do with me being a personal trainer..."

"I'm sorry..."

"Don't be – that was a long time ago..."

"Well you won't have to worry about a jealous boyfriend running up on you either – he broke up with me for something that had nothing to do with me having a personal trainer..."

"I'm sorry..."

"Don't be – he did me a favor..."

"How?"

"He taught me that the next man will be the right man..."

"Really?"

"Really..." I answered as I signed the last page and pushed the paperwork towards him...

"Can I ask you a personal question?" he asked as he began typing in my information...

"Sure..."

"Would you have dinner with me?"

"Not tonight..."

"So you'll have dinner with me another night?"

"I might..." I answered as I smiled...

"Okay – you're all set..." he said as he got up...

"When can I start?"

"You can start as soon as I grant you access..." he answered as he went over to a card reader, punched in a few numbers, swiped a card, and then handed it to me... "This is your temporary card – you'll get a permanent one the next time you come in – c'mon – I'll show you around..." he said as he took my hand and led me out to the reception area. I didn't bother letting go of his hand as he led me around the gym, showing me the nautilus equipment, free weights, treadmills, and elliptical riders. He continued to lead me towards the opposite end of the gym and when I saw the pool I got excited...

"Ooohhh – you have a pool!"

"And a Jacuzzi..."

"I might just come in here and go straight to the pool..."

"You won't be the only one..."

"Really?"

"Oh yea – we have members that pay to come in here to swim..."

"Where's the locker room?"

"Right this way..." he answered as he took me towards the locker room...

"This is bigger than I thought!" I exclaimed...

"We have clients that come here straight from work. They come in, change into their work out clothes, work out, come back here, shower if they want, change back into their clothes, and go home..."

"Do you have any private showers?" I asked as I looked around...

"Yes – the private showers are over here..." he answered as he took me to the other end of the locker room...

"I like the privacy – but how do I know no one can come in while I'm in there?"

"Take off your shoes..."

"Excuse me?"

"Take off your shoes..."

"Okay..." I sighed as I took them off...

"Go in there and close the door..."

"Okay – I'm in here – now what?"

"Now lock the door..." he laughed. I locked the door, unlocked the door, and came back out... "Still worried about someone coming in?"

"I guess not..." I sighed as I put my shoes back on...

"I'll walk you out..." he said as he took my hand and led me back out by the nautilus equipment. As soon as I saw Rashad sitting behind Angela, I knew he was more than her personal trainer...

"Stop..." she laughed as she looked back at Rashad...

"Thank you for changing your mind..." Randall said, interrupting my thoughts...

"Thank you for changing my mind..."

"You're welcome..."

"I'll see you soon..." I said as I left the gym.

Chapter 2

"Hey Clarisse..." Tasha greeted...

"Heeyy..." I sighed...

"Tisha! Get out here now!" Tasha exclaimed...

"What's wrong?" Tisha exclaimed as she hurried out into the hallway...

"Clarisse got tea!"

"Hold on – le'me lock my door..." Tisha said as she hurried back to her apartment, locked her door, and hurried back over to me... "Okay Clarisse – spill it!" she commanded...

"I don't know what you're talking about..."

"Oh shit – girl – you got some dick – didn't you?"

"Attention residents of the 2nd floor – I – Clarisse – did not get any dick!" I laughed...

"What are you yelling for?" Tasha laughed...

"Since you want everyone in my business, I figured I'd clear that up!" I laughed...

"I'm sorry – but did you?" Tasha asked...

"Come inside..." I laughed as I unlocked my door and they both pushed me inside...

"Spill it!" Tasha commanded...

"Can I sit down? Damn!" I laughed as they hurried over to the loveseat and put their hands under their chin... "I found a gym..." I said as I sat down...

"Girl – I'm out!" Tisha exclaimed as she went to get up but Tasha pulled her back down..."

"Tell us more about this gym..." Tasha said as she leaned forward...

"R & R..."

"Wai – a – min – did you say R & R?" Tisha asked...

"Yea – why?"

"Stay the fuck away from that gym!"

"Tisha!" Tasha exclaimed...

"Rashad & Randall – they get you to join – they seem really nice – and they are – until you refuse to fuck 'em!"

"Oh my God! Which one was it?!" I asked...

"Rashad..."

"Oh I know – he's a grimy mutha fucka..." I confirmed...

"You know?" Tasha asked...

"I felt it – it's not necessarily what he did – but when he touched my hand he made my skin crawl..."

"See?!" Tisha exclaimed...

"That's why I was leaving – and then Randall came over..."

"Ooohhh – now I see why you cheesing..." Tasha said...

"Clarisse – please be careful – Randall seems nice too – but after what happened with me and Rashad..."

"Oh my God..." I whispered...

"Relax – it wasn't that – trust me – I'd be in jail!" Tisha exclaimed...

"Tisha – why didn't you tell me?!" Tasha asked...

"There wasn't anything to tell..."

"So you stopped going for nothing?"

"I signed up, I started going. I wanted to tighten up a few areas so I hired Rashad as my personal trainer. He was alright at first – but then he got a little too touchy feely – and he'd say things like your ass is firming up nicely – and then he'd palm it – or he'd come up behind me when I was working out on the nautilus machine and put his hands on my waist – and have the nerve to get mad when I asked him to stop!"

"I saw him do that with Angela..." I said...

"Who's Angela?" Tisha asked...

"One of his clients..."

"Uh huh – did she make him stop?"

"She told him to stop – but she was laughing...

"He's probably fuckin' her..."

"I think so..."

"So are you going back to that gym?" Tasha asked...

"Yea..."

"After what I just told you?! Unfuckin' believable!" Tisha exclaimed...

"Tisha – I feel you as far as Rashad – but Randall was different..."

"Of course he was different – he did what he needed to do to get you to sign up – and then he got you on the hook to be your personal trainer – right?"

"Actually – no..."

"Uh huh – a new approach – he's gonna take his time with you..."

"Tisha – I get it – I'll be careful..."

"Please do – I wish I knew you were looking for a gym before you went down there..."

"As long as she stays away from Rashad she'll be fine..." Tasha said...

"Tasha – just because Randall seems nice – doesn't mean he is!"

"You don't have to get nasty!"

"Ladies – stop it – Tasha – your sister's just looking out for me – I'd do the same thing..."

"Exactly!" Tisha exclaimed...

"I hope you're wrong though..." I sighed...

"You like Randall?" Tasha asked...

"Hell yea!"

"Clarisse!" Tisha exclaimed...

"Tisha – I heard you – but when he smiled at me – I was done – and when he spoke – those lips..."

"He does have nice lips..." Tisha agreed...

"Wait, wait, wait – you just told her she needs to be careful!" Tasha exclaimed...

"She does – but I ain't gonna front – Randall is easy on the eyes..." Tisha said...

"I bet he's easy in other places too..." I sighed...

"Okay – that's it – I give up!" Tasha laughed...

"He asked me out to dinner..."

"What?!" they both exclaimed...

"I told him not tonight!" I laughed...

"So basically you said yes!" Tisha laughed...

"I told him I'd think about it..."

"She said yes..." Tasha laughed...

"Well – I need to get going – I need to have dinner ready when he gets home..." Tisha said as she got up...

"So do I..." Tasha said...

"One day..." I sighed as I got up to let them out...

"Please be careful..." Tisha said...

"I will..."

"Keep us posted..." Tasha said...

"You'll be the first to know..." I laughed as they left and my phone started ringing...

"R & R Gym..." I read out loud... "Hello..."

"Thanks for answering..."

"What can I do for you Randall?"

"You can have dinner with me tomorrow night..."

"Randall – I..."

"I know..." he interrupted... "You said you'd think about it – but tomorrow's our monthly happy hour..."

"You have a monthly happy hour?"

"There's a place downtown called HR Happy Hour. We treat our employees to happy hour once a month to show them we appreciate them and we invite our members to come. R & R members get two drinks for the price of one the entire evening, as well as a 10 percent discount on their meals..."

"Wow – that sounds so nice – are you hiring?"

"Not at the moment – but if you're serious, I'll keep you in mind..."

"Okay – I'll come to the gym tomorrow and we can go from there..."

"Okay – you'll see employees and you'll see some of my other clients – but after happy hour is over, I want us to have dinner..."

"Okay..."

"See you tomorrow..."

"See you tomorrow..." I said as I hung up and my 'Orgasmic Orchestra' began...

"Oh God... Fuck me... Yes..."
"You like that?"
"Yes...."
"Throw that ass back on this dick!"
"I'm 'bout to cum..."
"Cum for me!"
"Huh... Huh... Huh..."
"Uugh! Uugh! Uugh!"
"Huh... Huh... Huh..."
"Uugh! Uugh! Uugh!"
"Aaah! Aaah! Aaah!"
"Uugh! Uugh! Uugh!"
"Thud!"

I shook my head and laughed to myself as I went into the kitchen. When I first moved in, I was turned on the first time I heard Tasha fucking her boyfriend. These walls are so thin it felt as if I was in their bedroom with them. As soon as they started fucking, I'd turn down the volume on the television or the music, lie back on the couch, close my eyes, and breathe as if I were the one getting the dick. After Tisha moved in on the other side of me, things went in another direction. The first time I heard Tisha fucking her boyfriend they scared the shit outta me. I had fallen asleep in the living room on the couch and when they started fucking he was banging her so hard I thought they were going to come through my wall...

"Whose pussy is this?!"

"Yours! Oh God! Fuck me!"

"Uuugh! Uuugh! Uuugh!" With each thrust the headboard would bang against the wall so hard it rattled my stereo. I had to have a conversation with her the next day and it was really awkward...

"Hi – are you my neighbor?" she asked as she answered her door...

"Yes – I'm Clarisse..."

"I'm Tisha – come in..."

"Listen – I need to talk to you about something..."

"Oh God – you're not about to tell me you smell my weed are you? I had to leave my last apartment because the tenant complained..."

"No..."

"Is my music too loud?"

"No..."

"You hear me fuckin'?"

"Yea..."

"Well shit – I hope you didn't come over here to tell me to stop fuckin'!" she laughed...

"Can you come to my house?"

"Wai – a – min – I don't get down like that!"

"Oh my God – Nooo!" I laughed...

"Okay – sorry 'bout that – but you know..."

"C'mon..." I laughed as we left her apartment and went to mine...

"Oh this is nice – my bedroom is on the other side of your living room..."

"That's what I wanted to talk to you about..."

"I'm not gonna stop fuckin'..." she laughed...

"I know – I don't want you to – but..."

"Oh shit – we turn you on?"

"Nooo..." I laughed... "You rattle my television and my stereo..."

"Oh shit – I get it – when he's bangin' the headboard we bang the wall and it shakes your unit – can you move it to the other wall?"

"My couch won't fit under the window – I've already tried..." I sighed...

"I'll see if I can change my room around – maybe I can put my bed on the other wall – if it will fit..."

"If your bed doesn't fit on the other wall, you can always change the headboard..."

"You takin' me shopping for furniture?"

"Umm... No..."

"I didn't think so..." she laughed... "I'll see what I can do..."

"Thanks..."

"You don't have a man – do you?"

"No..."

"I didn't think so..."

"Why – because it's so quiet?"

"Basically..." she said and then we both laughed...

Fortunately for me, her bed fit on the other wall so I didn't have to worry about my unit anymore – but every night like clockwork they both treat me to the 'Orgasmic Orchestra' – and now that Tasha's finished, intermission is over, Tisha's about to start...

"You want this dick?"

"Yea..."

"Get down on your knees..."

"I might as well order some Chinese food..." I laughed...

"Hello, Hing Wong – pick up or delivery?"

"Delivery..."

"What would you like?"

"I'd like some Randall..." I thought to myself...

"Hello?"

"Oh – I'm sorry – I'd like a number 69!" I laughed...

"You want chicken & shrimp combination with white rice – large or small?"

"Yes... that's it... suck it..."

"Large!" I laughed...

"Okay – we use credit card you have on file – 45 minutes..."

"Okay – thank you..." I laughed as I hung up...

"Bring that ass here..."
"Oh God – Ron... Yes..."
"Uuugh! Uuugh! Uuugh!"
"Huh! Huh! Huh!"
"Gimmie that pussy!"
"Ron... Fuck... I'm cumming!"
"Uuugh! Uuugh! Uuugh! Uuugh! Uuugh!"
"Aaah! Aaah! Aaah! Aaah! Aaah!"

"Maybe I can watch a little HGTV before my food gets here..." I said out loud as I picked up the remote... "Love It or List It – perfect..." I sighed as I put the remote down and began to relax... "Oh – I don't want that house... No David – I don't like that one... Nice house – too far out... Are you seriously complaining about a 15 minute commute? Shut the hell up! Who is it?"

"Delivery!"

"I'll be right there!" I yelled as I got up and answered the door as Tisha and her man began round 2...

"They having good sex!" the deliveryman laughed as he handed me my food...

"Thank you – good night..." I said as I closed the door in his face... "So he really thought

I was going to stand there and talk to him about my fuckin' neighbors!" I laughed out loud as I opened the cartons, put the food on a plate, took a fork out the drawer, and went back into the living room...

"So are you going to Love It?"

"Or are you going to List It?"

"They're going to List It..." I answered as they played their anticipating music...

"We're going to List It!" the wife exclaimed...

"Good – you can have the other house – I'll take your house..." I said out loud as I continued eating.

Chapter 3

"**Hello** Clarisse..." Rashad greeted as I walked in...

"Hello Rashad – is Randall here?"

"He's in his office with another client – is there something I can help you with?"

"No thank you – I'll wait for Randall..."

"Suit yourself..." he said as I walked towards the locker room. When I got inside I hurried to a locker, changed out of my clothes, put my things in the locker, locked it, and went back towards the nautilus machines...

"Hello Clarisse..." Randall greeted...

"Hi Randall..." I greeted as I smiled at him. I saw Rashad was watching us and I paid it no mind...

"Happy Hour starts soon..."

"I know – listen – I know I didn't schedule an appointment with you – but could you do me a favor?"

"Sure..."

"Could you watch me work out and give me your opinion?"

"My opinion?"

"Yea – less of this, more of that, eliminate that..."

"Okay – sure..." he answered as he followed me over to the elliptical and I got on. I rode the elliptical for 10 minutes before I got off and went over to the nautilus machine. I sat down on the bench and when I grabbed the bar, he stopped me... "Wait a minute..."

"Yes?" He got behind me and sat down on the bench...

"Grab the bar again..."

"Okay..." I said as I grabbed the bar with both hands... "Move your hands here..." he said as he put his hands on top of mine and moved them...

"Okay..."

"Try it now..." I took his advice and it felt a little better...

"Better?"

"Yea – thanks..." I thought he was going to touch me around my waist – I wanted him to – but he didn't – instead he got up and observed me. When I was finished with my arms I laid back on the bench to do some leg presses and although he was watching me, he was focusing more on the amount of weight I was pushing and less on my legs, which put me at ease. After I was done with my legs, I reached up for the bar to bench press some free weights, but he stopped me...

"Let me take some of the weight off..." he laughed...

"I can do it..."

"I'm sure you can – but that doesn't mean you should..." he said as he took a few weights off on each side...

"Try it now..."

"It's too light..."

"Okay – I'll put a little more on – but I don't want you to go over 30 pounds..."

"Why?" I panted as I lifted the bar...

"Because you want to maintain your muscle – not continue to build on it..."

"Why shouldn't I continue to build on it?" I asked as I sat up...

"Because you look good just the way you are..." he answered as he smiled...

"Thank you..."

"You're welcome..."

"Randall – your 5:30 is here..." Rashad interrupted...

"Thank you Rashad – Clarisse – I'll see you later?"

"Yea..."

"Okay..." he said as he went to take care of his client...

"I thought you said my client was here..." Randall said as he walked out to the waiting area..."

"You hittin' that?" Rashad asked...

"Are you fuckin' serious right now?"

"Well? Are you?"

"Is my client here or not?"

"Your client isn't here yet – are you hittin' that or not?"

"No I'm not hittin' that..."

"Oh God – you still on that waitin' shit?"

"Yes – I'm still on that waitin' shit – and I'ma stay on that waitin' shit!"

"Whatever helps you sleep at night – I now pronounce you, Mary Palm, and her five sisters, husband and wives – tonight while you're on your waitin' shit honeymoon you can consummate your marriage! Aaa Haaa Haaa Haaa!"

"Shut the fuck Rashad!" Randall laughed...

"Okay – I'm a stop – for now – but real talk – you feelin' her?"

"Yea..."

"Oh shit – okay – that's what's up – you invite her to Happy Hour?"

"Yea..."

"Okay – maybe there's hope for you after all – she feelin' you too?"

"Yea..."

"Maybe you'll get lucky..."

"I'm not trying to get lucky..."

"Shit – why not?"

"Because I want more..."

"Hello Randall..." Demi greeted...

"Hello Demi..."

"Sorry I'm late..."

"That's okay – let's get started – Happy Hour starts as soon as I can get you there..." Randall said as he took Demi by the hand and led her into the gym. I sat on the bench and watched Randall with her for a few minutes and then I chastised myself...

"Clarisse – he's a personal trainer – he's doing his job..." After I finished chastising myself, I got up from the bench, went into the locker room, got my things, took a quick shower, and headed out towards HR Happy Hour...

"**Damn** – it's lit in here – okay!" I exclaimed as I walked inside. I went to sit at the bar because all the tables were taken...

"Hey Beautiful – buy you a drink?"

"Thank you for the compliment – but I'm waiting for a friend..."

"Friend my ass – bartender – get her whatever she wants – put it on my tab..."

"What'll it be?" the bartender asked...

"I'm not having anything until my friend gets here..."

"Your friend is here – now stop being a Bitch and let a man buy you a drink..."

"The lady said no..." Randall said as I turned around...

"Get the fuck off..."

"Uh uh – leave... now..."

"Oh shit – Randall – that's you?"

"That's me..."

"My bad – apologies..."

"You owe my lady an apology..."

"My apologies Beautiful..."

"Whatever..." I sighed...

"I'm sorry..." Randall sighed...

"Maybe I should go..."

"Please – don't leave – he turns into an ass whenever he drinks..."

"Oh so you mean he's not always an ass?" I laughed...

"C'mon on – I'll show you around..." he said as he held out his hand for me to take...

"Okay..." I relented. Randall showed me around the bar, introduced me to the Manager, and then I saw Rashad with Angela... "Are they dating?" I asked...

"Umm... oh look – a table!" he laughed as he pulled me towards it and sat me down in the chair...

"Okay!" I laughed as he sat down...

"Hello – what can I get you?" the hostess yelled over the music. Randall motioned for her to bend down so he could whisper in her ear. The hostess wrote something down on her pad and walked away... "Umm... excuse me?"

"Yes?"

"What if I don't like what you ordered for me?"

"You will..." he answered as he smiled at me...

"I better..." I said as I smiled back at him...

"Here's your drinks..." the hostess said as she put them on the table...

"Umm – there's four drinks here..." I laughed...

"Two for one..." the hostess said as she walked away...

"Thank you..." I said as I picked up my margarita...

"You're welcome..."

"How'd you know I like margaritas?"

"Lucky guess..."

"What are you drinking?"

"Henny..."

"Here's your food..." the hostess said as she placed a tray of beef & lobster tacos, potato skins with bacon & cheese, garlic parmesan wings, fried pork wontons, fried calamari, mozzarella sticks, and cheeseburger sliders on the table...

"Oh my God – I'm about to bust this down!" I exclaimed...

"Let me know if you need anything else..." the hostess said before she walked away...

"I'm glad you're happy..." Randall said...

"I am..."

"Take as much as you want..."

"Oh so this is a plate for two?" I laughed...

"Are you serious? I know you work out but..."

"I'm just playin'..." I laughed...

"You sure? If you're serious, I'ma watch you handle your business..." he laughed...

"Oh no you're not – we're going to share this plate of appetizers – and skip right to dessert!" I laughed...

"I like the sound of that..."

"Oh no – shit – that's not what I mean – I..."

"Relax – I know that's not what you meant..."

"I'm sorry – I'm not normally like this..."

"Like what?"

"Nervous..."

"Nervous? Why?"

"Nothing – never mind..." I said as I finished my first drink and started to help myself to some food...

"Uh uh – don't do that..."

"Do what?"

"Don't start something and tell me it's nothing..."

"I'm sorry..."

"Don't do that either..."

"Well sir – why don't you just tell me what you'd like me to do then?"

"I'd like you to tell me why you're nervous..."

"I'm nervous because... I'm feelin' you..."

"I'm nervous because... I'm feelin' you too..." We sat there and continued eating and drinking without speaking. Each time he put something in his mouth or licked his fingers, I thought about his lips and tongue on me...

"How's everything here?" the hostess asked...

"Fine..." I sighed...

"Would you like another drink?" she asked...

"I'll have some water..."

"How 'bout you?" she asked Randall...

"I'll have some water too..." he answered...

"Shall I bring over the dinner menu or would you like the check?"

"Are you still hungry?" Randall asked...

"No..."

"You can put the check on our account..."

"Okay – enjoy your evening..." the hostess said as she walked away. When she came back to the table with our water she gave Randall a receipt and he put it in his pocket...

"Tell me about R & R..." I said...

"We've been in business for 10 years..."

"Congratulations..."

"We've been friends since kindergarten..."

"Really?"

"Yea..."

"What made you go into business together?"

"That was always the plan..."

"Always?"

"We used to say we were going to get a business together because we didn't want to work for anyone..."

"Have you ever felt like... never mind..."

"Uh uh – don't do that..."

"Have you ever felt like you couldn't trust Rashad?"

"Never..."

"That's good..."

"We both went to Harvard and we both got our Masters in Business. One day Rashad saw the building and suggested we go into business together..."

"Whose idea was R & R?"

"That was his idea – he said let's name the gym R & R – it'll keep us humble..."

"I like that!" I exclaimed...

"I know he rubbed you the wrong way..."

"He's not my type..."

"So are you saying I'm your type?"

"I'm definitely feelin' you..."

"Tell me about you..."

"What would you like to know?"

"Everything..."

"I was born at 9:15 p.m. My mother was in labor for 10 hours before they gave her an epidural..."

"Stop!" he laughed...

"I'm a paralegal at Lawler & Freeman..." I laughed...

"You like being a paralegal?"

"Oh yea – I'm never bored – you'd be surprised what comes across my desk..."

"Care to share?"

"I'm sorry – I can't go into details – but between you and me – I recognized some of your clients..."

"Oh shit!"

"Sshh!"

"Sorry – I couldn't help it..." he laughed... "So do you have any friends?"

"Tisha and Tasha..."

"Sisters?"

"Yea..."

"I'm surprised you didn't invite them tonight..."

"I didn't want to..."

"Oh – it's like that?"

"Sometimes..."

"I can respect that..."

"Don't get me wrong – I love them – but sometimes I want to do me – and tonight – I wanted to do you..."

"You wanna do me?"

"Oh shit – I didn't mean it like that – I..."

"Relax!" he laughed...

"I just wanted you to myself tonight..." I sighed...

"You ready to get out of here?"

"Yea..."

"C'mon..." he said as he stood up and extended his hand. I stood up, took his hand, and we walked outside. Randall continued holding my hand as we walked towards Seaside Park. When we got there, he took me over to a bench, sat down, and invited me to sit down with him. As soon as I sat down, he put his arm around me and pulled me close to him, and I didn't object, but I did chastise myself...

"Clarisse – what are you doing?"

"I'm doing what I want to do..." I answered to myself as I put my arm around Randall's waist and sighed...

"Can I kiss you?"

"Yes..." Randall kissed me softly and sensually for a few minutes and then he spoke...

"Come home with me..."

"I'm not ready for that..."

"Oh shit – I didn't mean it like that – I..."

"Relax!" I laughed...

"I asked you to have dinner with me – I'm a man of my word – let me cook for you..."

"It's getting late – can I take you up on that another night?"

"How 'bout tomorrow?"

"Tomorrow's fine..." I sighed...

"I'll walk you home..." he said as he got up...

"Okay..." I sighed as I took his hand and we walked toward Lafayette Street. When we got to my building, he tried to kiss me goodnight and I stopped him...

"Something wrong?"

"Yes..."

"Did I do something to offend you?"

"It's not what you did – it's what you didn't do..."

"I don't understand..."

"You said you were going to walk me home..."

"You don't live here?"

"I live in this building..." I answered...

"Oh – okay – let me get the door for you!" he exclaimed as he laughed...

"Thank you..." I said as we went inside...

"Good evening Clarisse..."

"Good evening Charles..." I greeted as I went towards the elevator with Randall following behind me. When we got to the elevator I pushed the button and we got in...

"What floor?"

"2nd..." Randall pushed the button and we didn't say anything until we got off the elevator...

"I'm home..." I announced as we got in front of my apartment door...

"Can I kiss you goodnight?"

"Yes..." I breathed as I pulled him into a kiss... "Oh shit – c'mon!" I exclaimed as I heard Tisha in the elevator...

"What's wrong?"

"I'll tell you inside – c'mon!" I exclaimed as I unlocked the door and pushed him inside...

"What's going on?"

"Sit down..."

"Okay..." Randall sighed as he went to sit down on the loveseat. I sat down beside him and he took my hand... "What's wrong?"

"That was Tisha..."

"Your friend?"

"Yea..."

"I see..." he said as he let go of my hand...

"No..." I said as I took his hand... "You don't..."

"Make me understand then..."

"After I met you I told them about you..."

"Is that right?"

"Yes..."

"So you really are feelin' me..."

"Yes..."

"Okay – we can keep us a secret for now..." he said as he tried to kiss me again...

"Randall – wait..."

"What's wrong?"

"Please don't tell Rashad..."

"What's Rashad got to do with this?!"

"Tisha told me she stopped going to the gym because of Rashad..."

"Are you telling me Rashad did something to Tisha?"

"Tisha said Rashad got mad because she wouldn't have sex with him..."

"Dammit!"

"Please don't tell Rashad!"

"I won't tell Rashad..." he sighed...

"You're mad at me..."

"I'm not mad at you..." he sighed... "I'm mad at Rashad..."

"I'm sorry..."

"Thank you for telling me..." he said as he got up to leave...

"Are we still on for tomorrow?" I asked as I got up...

"Oh yea..." he breathed as he pulled me into a kiss... "Good night..."

"Good night..." I sighed as he left right before the nightly 'Orgasmic Orchestra' began, starting with Tasha...

"Oh God... Fuck me... Yes..."

"You like that?"

"Yes...."

"Throw that ass back on this dick!"

"I'm 'bout to cum..."

"Cum for me!"

"Huh... Huh... Huh..."

"Uugh! Uugh! Uugh!"

"Huh... Huh... Huh..."

"Uugh! Uugh! Uugh!"

"Aaah! Aaah! Aaah!"

"Uugh! Uugh! Uugh!"

"Thud!"

Instead of waiting in the living room for the 2nd act to begin, I decided to go in the bedroom. After I got in the bedroom I got undressed, got in the bed, closed my eyes, and imagined Randall was making me scream his name as Tisha was screaming...

"You want this dick?"

"Yea..."

"Get down on your knees..."

"Yes... that's it... suck it... Bring that ass here..."

"Oh God – Ron... Yes..."

"Uuugh! Uuugh! Uuugh!"

"Huh! Huh! Huh!"

"Gimmie that pussy!"

"Ron... Fuck... I'm cumming!"

"Uuugh!   Uuugh!   Uuugh!   Uuugh! Uuugh!"

"Aaah! Aaah! Aaah! Aaah! Aaah!"

"Whose pussy is this?!"

"Yours! Oh God! Fuck me!"

"Uuugh! Uuugh! Uuugh!"

Chapter 5

"Hey Randall..."

"Hey Rashad – are you free right now?"

"I have some time – what's up?"

"Come in my office..."

"Oh shit – what'd I do now?" Rashad laughed as he followed Randall inside the office and sat down...

"Are you fuckin' Angela?"

"Well damn – what – are you my father?"

"I'm not tryin' na be..."

"Yea – shorty let me hit it – why?"

"Isn't she married?"

"I know you not about to try and lecture me..."

"No – I'm not – never mind..."

"Yea – she's married – what's with all the questions?"

"Did you ever sleep with a client that's available?"

"Randall – what's with all the fuckin' questions?"

"Okay – don't start – I'm feelin' Clarisse..."

"I know that!" Rashad laughed...

"I took her home last night..."

"Oh shit! Finally! Details!"

"It wasn't like that..."

"See – here we go – why are you waitin' – oh – le'me guess – she told you she ain't ready – right?"

"Yea..."

"But you wanted to fuck her?"

"Why you gotta be so harsh – I don't wanna fuck her just to fuck her – I'm really feelin' her..."

"See – you want a relationship – I just want pussy – that's the difference between me and you..."

"So you never take no for an answer?"

"I'm Rashad – I gets mine – ya heard me?"

"What's that supposed to mean?!"

"Calm down Randall – I'm a grimy mutha fucka – but I'm not a grimy mutha fucka – for every shorty that says no, there's a shorty that says yes – and that's the shorty I'ma rock with..."

"Okay – I feel better now..."

"Did somebody tell you something different about me?!"

"No – but..."

"But what?!"

"Please calm down..."

"Okay – I'm calm – now talk!"

"I took Clarisse home last night..."

"Okay – and?"

"So I went to kiss her goodnight and she stopped me..."

"See – I would've left her ass standin' there lookin' stupid..."

"Rashad – listen!"

"Aiight – go 'head!"

"So I asked her why she stopped me and she says she doesn't live outside – she lives in the building, upstairs..."

"Oh okay – shorty feelin' you too – I'm startin' to like her..."

"I went to give her a kiss goodnight and she rushed me inside because she heard Tisha coming..."

"Man – fuck her!"

"What happened with you and Tisha?"

"Tisha was feelin' me on the low – I wasn't really feelin' her but I like pussy and she was with it, so I hit it..."

"Oh my God – I don't believe you did that..."

"You tryin'a judge me?"

"Rashad – I'm not judging you – you said you weren't really feelin' her so..."

"So you think I should 'a turned down the pussy!" Rashad laughed...

"Well... yea..."

"See – that's you – that ain't me!"

"So that's why she stopped coming to the gym?"

"Randall – I'ma ask you again – did somebody tell you something?"

"Nobody told me anything – I was just surprised to see her and the way you're responding lets me know things didn't end well..."

"Look – she got mad because after I hit it, I told her I wasn't really feelin' her like that – then she tells me she's going to press charges on me for raping her..."

"Rashad!"

"Calm down – you see I'm here – right?!"

"You right..."

"She stopped poppin' her shit when I told her I had a video..."

"What?! You have a video?!"

"Yea..."

"Rashad! You can't video our clients – or anybody else for that matter! We've worked too hard for this!"

"Randall – who the fuck you think you talkin' too?"

"You!"

"Guess again – I'm not one of these stupid mutha fuckas we ran the street with in college that's still in the street – I would never do anything to jeopardize our business – I shouldn't even have to tell you that man!"

"You're right – I'm sorry..."

"Apology accepted..."

"So tell me about these videos – you ever tape you and Angela?"

"Mind your business!" Rashad laughed...

"I've never done that..."

"Are you sure you're not a virgin?" Rashad laughed...

"I'm not a virgin!" Randall laughed...

"When's the last time you got some pussy?"

"It's been months..."

"What the fuck – you never went out – met a girl – and hooked up for the night?!"

"I don't wanna do that anymore – I'm..."

"Don't even say it – I'm gonna get you some pussy – I can't take this shit anymore!" Rashad laughed...

"I don't need you to do that – I can do that myself..." Randall laughed...

"You got one more time to tell me you want pussy and you didn't get it..." Rashad laughed...

"Yo – you threatenin' me with pussy – I can't!" Randall laughed...

"I'm serious!" Rashad laughed...

"I know..." Randall laughed... "But what am I gonna do about Tisha?"

"You don't have to do a damn thing about Tisha! You didn't fuck her!"

"She's friends with Clarisse..."

"So what – if it bothers you that much – just invite Clarisse over to your place..."

"She'll be there tomorrow night..."

"Okay playa! I see you!" Rashad laughed...

Chapter 6

"Are you ready Clarisse?" Randall asked...

"I'll be ready in a few – I just need to take a shower..."

"You can always – never mind..."

"Uh uh – don't do that!"

"Okay – I'm sorry – my bad..." he laughed...

"What were you going to say?"

"Sigh... okay – I was going to say you could always take a shower at my place..."

"Okay..."

"Never mind – I don't know why I said that – wait a minute – what did you say?"

"I said okay!" I laughed...

"Really?"

"Really..."

"Are you sure?"

"You change your mind?"

"No – I haven't changed my mind – let's go!" he exclaimed as he grabbed my hand...

"Randall – wait!" I laughed...

"I'm sorry... I shouldn't have grabbed you like that..."

"I just need to get my things out of the locker – I'll be right back..." I said as I went to the locker room...

"Oh shit – shorty takin' a shower at your place!" Rashad exclaimed...

"Keep your voice down!"

"That's a good look – you might be gettin' some pussy tonight after all..."

"It's not about that..."

"You so full of shit – you know you want some pussy..." Rashad laughed...

"Yea... I do..."

"See?"

"I never said I didn't want pussy – I do – I just want it from her..."

"What'd I tell you? Didn't I tell you you had one more time to tell me you want pussy and you not getting' any?"

"I'll be gettin' plenty – when she's ready..."

"What if she tells you she wants to wait until she's married?"

"Then I'll marry her – and you'll be my best man..."

"Damn – I hope she's worth the wait..."
"She is Rashad... she is..."

"Oh my God..." I whispered as I started crying...
"Clarisse – there you are – Oh my God – what's wrong?"
"Nothing..." I answered as I wiped my eyes...
"Uh uh – don't do that – what's wrong?"
"Nothing..." I breathed as I pulled him into a kiss...
"You ready?"
"Yea..."
"C'mon..." he said as he took my hand and led me out...

"Oh wow..." I exclaimed as we walked into his luxury condo...
"Make yourself comfortable..."
"Randall – I don't want to sit on your furniture – I really need to take a shower..."
"Have a drink with me..."
"Okay..."
"I have beer, wine, and Henny..."
"What are you having?"
"Henny..."
"I'll have some wine I guess..."
"You want something else?"
"I like Captain Morgan..."
"I'll be right back..."

"Where are you going?"

"I'm going to get you some Captain Morgan..." he said as he snatched his keys and flew out the door...

"I guess I can look around until he gets back..." I sighed as I went down the hall... "Ooohhh..." I exclaimed as I saw the guest bathroom. It was large enough to dance around in. The walls were a bright yellow with glass-mosaic tiles lining the walk-in shower up to the ceiling. The shower had a large rain head as well as jets... "If this is the guest bathroom, I can only imagine what the master bath looks like..." I said as I went further down the hall and saw the guest bedroom... "This is nice..." I said as I looked inside the room. The room was decorated similar to the way the rooms are decorated at the Marriot with cream, red, and brown pillows, blankets, and comforters. I went to the end of the hall and I wasn't ready for what I saw. I fell in love with the ambience of the black king-size bed with the King & Queen of Spades above the headboard on the wall. I went into the bedroom and when I saw the master bathroom, I gasped... "Oh my God! This is beautiful!" The walk-in shower was built for two with two shower heads and two sets of jets, and was completely lined with pale blue glass mosaic tile. The sinks were glass as well and when I stepped into the bathroom, the heated floors warmed my feet... "I'm taking my shower in here..." I said as I stripped out of my sweaty gym clothes and got in the shower...

"Clarisse? Clarisse – where are you?" Randall called out... "Hmm – maybe she's in the bathroom..." he said as he started to come down the hall... "There you are..." he whispered as he tip-toed into the bedroom... "Oh my God... I'd give anything to be that loofah right now..." he whispered as I ran it all over my body and between my legs... "Damn this is hard..." he whispered as he put his hands between his legs and began stroking himself... "Uh uh – le'me go make this food..." he said as he tip-toed out of the bedroom, unaware that I knew he was watching me...

"That smells so good..." I said as I walked into the kitchen and sat down at the island...
"It will be..."
"What are you making?"
"You'll see..."
"Okay..."
"Here..." he said as he handed me a drink..."
"Thank you..."
"You're welcome..."
"I'll make sure I keep Captain Morgan on deck..." he said as he smiled at me...
"Stop it!" I told my clit – but I might as well have said go 'head 'cause she was calling his

mouth... "Need any help?" I asked as I got up and went over to him...

"You smell good..." he breathed as he pulled me close to him and kissed me...

"I don't want to shower at the gym anymore..."

"You don't have too..." he breathed in my ear and then he began kissing me on my neck...

"Is that chicken contadina?" I asked, hoping I could distract him...

"Yes..." he breathed as he continued kissing me on my neck... "It is..." I looked over at the counter and saw the Italian sausage, fresh peepers, onions, and dry vermouth and I thought of something in the nick of time...

"So..." I said as I pulled away from him... "What are we having with it?" Randall pulled me back into his arms and answered me in between kisses...

"We're... having... linguini... with... garlic... and... oil..."

"Mmm..." I moaned at the sound of the food and the feel of his lips...

"We're... " he breathed in my ear as he nibbled my ear lobe... "Also..." he breathed as he kissed my neck... "Having..." he breathed as he kissed my shoulder... "Salad!" he exclaimed as he pulled me to him and positioned my body so I could feel his dick pressing against me...

"Randall..."

"Yeesss..." he breathed as he kissed me...

"The water..."

"What about it?"

"It's... boiling..."

"So am I..." he breathed as he kissed me again before letting me go so he could put the linguini in the pot. I took the opportunity to get away from him and sat down at the dining room table. We both knew I wasn't going to be able to hold out much longer and he was going to find out later on tonight that I was okay with that... "Dinner's ready..."

"Good – 'cause I'm hungry..."

"So am I..." he said as he made two plates of salad and put them on the table. I watched him make the plates of linguini and chicken Contadina and when he brought them to the table I was in awe...

"Oh my God – that looks so good..."

"It will be..." he said as he went to get a bottle of white wine, opened it, poured two glasses, brought them to the table, and sat down...

"How'd you know this dish is one of my favorites?"

"I didn't..."

"Oh wow..."

"If it wasn't – it would've been after tonight..." he said as he picked up some food on his fork and put it in his mouth. When he licked the fork with his tongue before putting some more food on it, I knew I was in trouble...

"That was delicious – thank you..."

"You're welcome..."

"Do you need me to help you clean up?"

"I got it..." he said as he got up from the table. I watched him intently as he cleaned up everything, put the dishes in the dishwasher, and set it...

"You're going to run the dishwasher while you walk me home?" The look on Randall's face when he turned around was priceless...

"Yea..." he sighed. I knew he was disappointed, but he had no idea what was in store for him...

Unfortunately for me, as soon as we got off the elevator, I realized the nightly 'Orgasmic Orchestra' started early...

"Oh God... Fuck me... Yes..."

"Umm... who is that?" Randall laughed...

"That's Tasha..." I whispered...

"You like that?"

"Yes...."

"Do they do this all the time?" Randall asked as I unlocked my door...

"Every night..." I answered as I started to open the door but he stopped me...

"Wait..."

"Why?"

"Ssshhh..." he said as he put his finger to his lips and smiled at me...

"Okay..." I whispered as we continued listening...

"Throw that ass back on this dick!"

"I'm 'bout to cum..."

"Cum for me!"

"Huh... Huh... Huh..."

"Uugh! Uugh! Uugh!"

"Huh... Huh... Huh..."

"Uugh! Uugh! Uugh!"

"Aaah! Aaah! Aaah!"

"Uugh! Uugh! Uugh!"

"Thud!"

"That was quick..." Randall laughed...

"Don't worry – Tisha's getting ready to start..." I whispered as the intermission ended and Tisha began...

"You want this dick?"

"Yea..."

"Get down on your knees..."

"Oh... okay!" Ronald exclaimed...

"Sshhh!" I whispered as I put my hand over my mouth to keep from laughing...

"Yes... that's it... suck it... bring that ass here..."

"Oh God – Ron... Yes..."

"Uuugh! Uuugh! Uuugh!"

"Huh! Huh! Huh!"

"Damn - I guess she's over Rashad huh?" Randall laughed as we continued listening...

"Ssshhh!"

"Gimmie that pussy!"

"Ron... Fuck... I'm cumming!"

"Uuugh! Uuugh! Uuugh! Uuugh! Uuugh!"

"Aaah! Aaah! Aaah! Aaah! Aaah!"

"Whose pussy is this?!"

"Yours! Oh God! Fuck me!"

"Uuugh! Uuugh! Uuugh!"

"Oh yea – she's over Rashad..." he laughed as I opened the door and we went inside...

Chapter 7

As soon as we got in the door he pulled me into a kiss... "Mmmm..." he breathed as he kissed me. I knew he wanted me... and I wanted him too... but I was still afraid... "Don't be afraid... I won't hurt you..."

"I know..." I breathed as we continued kissing...

"Clarisse..."

"Yes Randall?"

"Do you want me?"

"Yes..."

"I don't understand... if you want me... then why..."

"Because he hurt me..." I interrupted...

"Who?"

"Darryl..." I sighed...

"What happened?" he asked as he led me to the couch and we sat down...

"I wanted to wait..."

"Okay..."

"He said he understood... so we waited..."

"Okay..."

"One night I told him I was ready..."

"Okay...

"We made love..."

"Okay..."

"After we made love..." I said before I started tearing up...

"Clarisse..." he whispered as he kissed my eyes and my tears... "What happened?"

"He said 'bout time you gave me some pussy..." I answered as I started crying...

"Ssshhh... don't cry..." he whispered as he kissed my lips, pulled me into a hug, and held me... "What happened after that?"

"He... got... dressed... and... he... left..." I cried...

"He bounced?"

"Yea..." I sniffed...

"Baby... I'm sorry..."

"I loved him..."

"He didn't deserve you..."

"I felt so stupid..."

"Listen to me..." he said as he picked up my face in his hands and kissed me... "You were not the stupid one – he was – understand?"

"Okay..."

"Clarisse... I love you..."

"I love you too..."

"You do?"

"Yes..."

"Say it again..." he breathed as he kissed me...

"I love you Randall...

"Again..."

"I... love... you... Randall..." I laughed between kisses...

"I... love... you... too... Clarisse..." he breathed... "And... I'll wait... as long... as... you... want... me... to..."

"I don't wanna wait anymore..." I breathed as I kissed him hard...

"Are you sure?"

"Yes..." Randall didn't say anything. He stood up, took my hand, helped me up off the couch, led me into the bedroom, sat down on the bed, and pulled me down beside him...

"Tell me you want me..." he breathed in my ear as he laid me down on the bed...

"I want you Randall..." I moaned as he started kissing my neck and squeezing my breasts...

"Tell me again..." he said as he put his hand in my jeans, spread my lips, and started rubbing my clit...

"I... want... you... Randall..." I moaned. Randall got up on his knees, lifted me up off the bed, pulled off my jeans, and looked down at me.

I watched as Randall took off his shirt, open his jeans, slid them off his ass along with his boxers, and pushed them off his legs as his dick sprung to attention. Randall smiled as I watched him stroke his dick...

"Tell me again..." he breathed...

"I want you Randall..." I panted. Randall came over to me, spread my legs apart, lay down on top of me, and kissed me as he unbuttoned my blouse and opened it...

"Tell me again..." Randall breathed as he leaned over me, reached in the drawer of the night stand, and pulled out a pair of scissors...

"I want you Randall..." I breathed as he cut my bra, put the scissors on the night stand, climbed on top of me, took my breasts in his mouth, and alternated between sucking the left and the right...

"Randall..." I moaned...

"Again... Mmmm..."

"I want you..."

"I want you too..." he breathed as he pushed my legs apart, slid down between my legs, spread my lips, and pulled my clit into his mouth...

"Randall... Huh..."

"Mmm..."

"Oh God... Randall... Randall... Randall..." I moaned as I arched my back and he put his hands up under my ass as I rode his face...

"Randall... Oh God... don't stop..." I moaned as I

began grinding my hips... "Randall... I'm cumming... I'm cumming... Aaaaahhhh!" Randall continued to suck on my clit softly as I rode out my orgasm and after a few mini-gasms, he came up between my legs and eased himself inside me slowly... and I gasped...

"Randall..." I moaned...

"Yesss... Clarisse..." he breathed in my ear as he wrapped his arm underneath my back and held me as he started thrusting... and I cried... "Clarisse... Baby... am I hurting you?"

"Nooo..." I cried...

"Are you sure?"

"Yeess..." I cried. Randall continued making love to me slowly as he began stroking me deeper... "Randall... Randall... Randall..." I moaned as tears streamed down my face...

"Clarisse... I love you..." he breathed as he kissed my eyes, my tears, and then my mouth...

"Hmmmm... Hmmmm... Hmmmm..."

"Mmph... Mmph... Mmph..." I dug my nails in his back as I started meeting his thrusts... "Clarisse... Clarisse... Clarisse..."

"Randall... Randall... Randall..." I moaned as Randall turned me on my left side and stroked me deeper..." "Randall... Randall... Randall... Oh God..." Randall kissed me hard, quickened his pace and stroked me harder... "HMMMMPH! HMMMMPH! HMMMMPH!" I moaned as Randall pushed his tongue in my mouth and came right behind me...

"HMMPH! HMMPH! HMMPH! HHHMMMPPPHHH!" he moaned in my mouth as he came...

"Randall..." I whispered...

"Clarisse..." he whispered as he cried...

"I love you Randall..." I breathed as I pulled his face to mine and kissed his tears and then his mouth...

"I've wanted you for so long..." he whispered as he started crying again...

"I'm sorry..." I breathed as I kissed him...

"You don't need to be sorry... I love you so much..." he cried...

"I love you too..." I whispered as I started crying again. We continued crying and kissing each other for a few moments... and then...

"Oh shit... I left something in the car... I need to go..." he said as he jumped up...

"Randall... Noooo..." I cried as I sat up in the bed and put my face in my hands...

"Clarisse..." Randall said as he sat down beside me on the bed and took my hands away from my face...

"Yes Randall?" I answered through tear-soaked eyes...

"I'm not Darryl..." he said and then he took my face in his hands and kissed me...

"So you're not leaving me?"

"No Baby... I'm not leaving you..." he answered as he kissed me again...

"You promise?"

"Clarisse... do you trust me?"

"I want to..."

"Tell me..."

"I... trust you Randall..."

"Tell me again..." he breathed as he kissed me...

"I... trust... you... Randall..." I breathed in between kisses...

"That's more like it..." he said and then he kissed me again... "Now... I want... you... to wait... right there... I'll be... right back..." he said as he got up, put on his shirt, put on his pants, threw on his jacket... and ran out the door...

"He must be coming back..." I said out loud... "He didn't even put his shoes on..." I laughed nervously... "Oh God... please let him come back..." I prayed...

"Shit!" Randall cursed as he started rummaging through his car. He searched the glove compartment frantically, throwing all the papers on the floor... "Where the fuck is it?" he growled as he checked the sun visors... "Oh God – please let me find it!" he pleaded...

"It's right there..." God whispered...

"Here it is – thank you Lord!" he breathed as he snatched the box up off the floor, jumped out the car, slammed the door, and ran back to the building... "Hold that door – please!" he yelled in desperation as the visitor was about to let the door close...

"Aiight man – I gotchu..." the visitor said as Randall caught up to the visitor...

"Thank you..." Randall panted...

"You're welcome..." The visitor laughed as he held the door open for Randall and Randall ran upstairs...

"Clarisse! Open the door!" Randall yelled...

"I'm coming!" I yelled as I jumped up out the bed, grabbed my robe, threw it on, ran to the door, and opened it...

"Clarisse..."

"Randall... what's wrong?" Randall took off his coat, dropped down on one knee... and opened the box... "Randall..." I whispered as I started crying...

"Clarisse..." Randall said as he started crying... "I love you so much... I don't wanna wait another minute... Will you marry me? Please?"

"Yes Randall... Yes..." I cried as he put the ring on my finger. Randall stood up, pulled me into a kiss, and kicked off his pants. I slid his shirt off his shoulders as we continued kissing and he slid my robe off my shoulders... "Randall..." I gasped as he picked me up by my ass and held me up as I wrapped my legs around his back. Randall carried me into the bedroom and we fell back on the bed and Randall thrust himself inside me while my legs were still wrapped around him... "Randall!" I screamed as he started pounding my pussy...

"Uuugh!   Uuugh!   Uuugh!   Uuugh! Uuugh!"

"Aaagh! Aaagh! Aaagh! Aaagh! Aaagh!"

"Damn – who the fuck is that?" Tasha laughed in the hallway...

"Clarisse..." Tisha laughed...

"Oh shit!" Tasha laughed as they got closer to the apartment door and continued listening...

"Uuugh! Uuugh! Uuugh! Uuugh!

"Damn – he make me wanna go fuck the shit outta my man!" Tasha said...

"I know – right?" Tisha laughed as they high-fived and continued listening...

"Randallllll!!! I'm cummingggg!!"

"UUUGH! UUUGH! UUUGH! UUUGH! UUUUGGGGHHHH!"

"Damn – I need my man to put it on me like that!" Tasha said...

"Shit – I need Randall to put it on me like that!" Tisha laughed...

"Girl!" Tasha laughed... "You aint' right!"

"I'm fine – he's the one that ain't right!"

"Baby – who you talkin' to – oh hey Tasha..."

"Hey Ron – le'me go girl – I'll see you later..." Tasha said as she hurried away from my apartment door. Tisha walked towards Ron with her head down. Ron took Tisha by the hand... led her into their apartment... and closed the door....

"Tisha?"

"Yes Ron?" she answered cautiously..."

"I heard what you said..."

"You... you did?" she stuttered...

"I did..." Ron said as he walked over to her... pulled her into a kiss... and kissed her hard...

"Ron... I..."

"Come with me..." he said as he took her by the hand and led her into the bedroom... "Take off your clothes..." Tisha did as she was told and stood there naked... "Get on the bed..." Tisha got on the bed on her back and spread her legs. Ron climbed up on the bed... picked up Tisha's legs... put them on his shoulders... and thrust himself inside her...

"ROOONNNN!" she screamed...

"That's right – scream my name... UUUGH!" he growled...

"RON! FUCK ME! YES! YES!"

"Is this what you want?" he growled as he pounded her...

"YES! OH GOD!"

"Is this God's pussy... or mine?"

"YOURS!"

"Damn right it is!" he growled...

"It sounds like we inspired them..." Randall laughed as we continued kissing...

"I think you're right…" I laughed…

"You ever heard them fucking before?"

"Yea – but I've never heard them fucking like that…"

"Mmmm… so he's competing… with me…"

"He could never compete with you…"

"How do you know?"

"I've lived here for months – I've never heard him fuck her like that…"

"So…" he said as he kissed me… "What you're saying is…" he said as he kissed me again… "I'm good…"

"Yeesss…"

"Le'me ask you something…"

"Okay…"

"Did you imagine what I'd feel like?"

"Yeesss…" I breathed…

"Did you ever fantasize about me making love to you?" he asked as he began kissing my neck…

"Yeesss…" I moaned…

"Did you ever touch yourself while you were fantasizing about me making love to you?" he asked as he reached between my legs and started playing with my clit…

"Randall… Yeesss…" I moaned…

"Tell me…"

"I held your dick in my hand…" I said as I started stroking his dick…

"Clarisse…" he moaned…

"You pushed me on the bed... Huh..." I moaned...

"Tell me..."

"You spread my legs..."

"Like this?" he breathed as he got on top of me and spread my legs...

"Yes... like that..." I breathed...

"Did I make love to you..." he breathed in my ear... or..." he asked as he slid himself inside me... "Did I fuck you?"

"Oh Randall..." I moaned...

"Answer me..." he growled as he fucked me harder...

"You... Fucked...Me... Haagh..."

"Mmmm... that's what I thought..." he growled as he fucked me harder and deeper...

"Randall..." I moaned as I dug my nails in his ass...

"Clarisse... Fuck..."

"I'm cumming... I'm cumming... I'm cumming..."

"I'm cumming... with... you... Uuggh! Uuggh! Uuggh! Uuggh! UUUGGGHHHH!"

"Maybe I should've made you wait a little longer..." I laughed...

"That wasn't happening..." he laughed...

"You're pretty sure of yourself..." I said and then he kissed me...

"I'm sure of you..." he breathed as he kissed me...

"I don't understand..."

"You wanted me..."

"Yes... I wanted you..."

"You fantasized about me fucking you..."

"Yes... I did..."

"You were ready for me..."

"I was..."

"Did your fantasy come true?"

"Yes Randall... Yes..."

"So did mine..."

"Oh Randall..."

"I closed my eyes and stroked myself just about every night... fantasizing I was fucking you..."

"Oh Randall... am I everything you dreamed of?"

"No..."

"I'm not?"

"No... You're more than I imagined..."

"Randall... I love you..."

"I love you too Clarisse..."

"I guess you can tell Rashad I finally gave you some pussy..." I laughed...

"Fuck him..."

"What?"

"I said fuck him..."

"But I thought...

"This ain't none of his fuckin' business..." he said as he eased himself back inside me again... "This is our fuckin' business... he breathed as he started fucking me again...

Chapter 8

"Hey Clarisse..."

"Hey Rashad..."

"Listen – Randall wants you to meet him at my place tonight..."

"Really?"

"Yea – here..." he said as he gave me a piece of paper...

"What's this?"

"My address..."

"Let me call Randall and..."

"No!"

"Why?"

"Look – he has a surprise for you – don't make me ruin it – okay?"

"Okay!" I squealed...

"See you around 6:30?"

"I'll be there at 6:30!" I squealed as I hurried out the door...

"Hey Rashad..." Randall answered...
"Hey – listen – can you come by tonight around 7?"
"What's wrong?"
"I need to talk to you..."
"Why don't you come by my place instead?"
"Randall!"
Aiight – I'll be there at 7..." Randall said as he hung up...
"Perfect..." Rashad said as he smiled a sinister smile...

"I wonder what the surprise is?" I asked out loud as I jumped in the shower. I took the quickest shower I've ever taken and went into the bedroom to get dressed... "I guess he told Rashad we're engaged..." I said out loud as I hurried out...

"I swear to God – he better not be on any bullshit..." Randall said as he got up... "I plan on spending the night with Clarisse – he better make it quick – whatever it is..." Randall said as he grabbed his keys and headed out...

"Come in Clarisse..." Rashad said as he opened the door...
"Thank you – is Randall here yet?"
"He'll be here in a few – go on upstairs..."

"Why do I need to go upstairs?"

"Clarisse – please – don't make me spoil the surprise – go upstairs – okay?"

"Okay..." I sighed as I went upstairs and Randall followed behind me. When I got to the top of the stairs, I got a bad feeling... "I'm gonna go back downstairs until Randall gets here..." I said as I turned and tried to go back downstairs...

"C'mere Bitch!" Rashad growled as he grabbed me by my hair, threw me down on the floor, and held me down...

"Nooo! Get off me!" I screamed...

"Scream all you want – nobody's gonna give a damn!" he laughed maniacally as he ripped my shirt open...

"Nooo! Stop!" I cried...

"I'll stop... when I'm done with you..." he breathed as he pinned me down on the floor and forced my legs open. I was crying hysterically and I could see he was enjoying it... "Yes... fight me... I like that shit..." he breathed as he held me down by my throat with one hand and unzipped my jeans with the other...

"Get... off... me..." I managed to choke out..."

"I said..." he growled in my ear... "I'll stop when I'm done..."

"Please... don't do this..." I cried as he pulled off my jeans and panties...

"I haven't done anything... yet..." he said as he spread my legs... "Mmmm... nice..." he said as he smiled maniacally... "Where the hell do you think you're going?" he asked as I tried to get away from him and he grabbed me by my throat and shoved me up against the wall...

"I... I..."

"See... it didn't have to be like this..." he said as he held me against the wall by my throat... "But you don't wanna give up the pussy... and I've run outta patience..."

"But... you're his best friend..." I cried as he turned me face forward, pushed my face into the wall, ripped my shirt off, and ripped my bra...

"Yes – I'm his best friend – and I'm sick of hearing him complain..." he growled as he pushed my bra off my shoulders and turned me back around to face him...

"Wwhhaatt?" I stuttered...

"This shit's gon' stop – you gon' give him some pussy – and you gon' give it to him... tonight..." he breathed in my ear as he pushed himself up against me and ran his hand over my breast before he squeezed it...

"Please... don't..." I cried...

"Bitch please – I'on wantchu – I'on even know why he wants you – it's not like you all that..." he laughed. I slumped down onto the floor and sobbed...

"Bitch – get up!" he growled as he grabbed me by my hair and began pulling me towards the bed...

"Nooo! Let go of me!" I screamed to no avail as I tried to stop him from dragging me across the room...

"Get your ass on the fuckin' bed!" he growled as he threw me down on the bed and threw himself down on top of me...

"Help! Somebody please! Help me!" I screamed as he grabbed my left wrist and handcuffed me to the bed...

"Don't worry..." he said as he bent down and whispered in my ear... "He's on his way..."

"I... I... I don't understand..." I sobbed...

"I already called him..."

"Why?"

"Like I said – this shit gon' stop – you gon' give him some pussy – and you gon' give it to him tonight..." he said as he smiled at me manically...

"He told you to do this?" I asked as I moved up on the bed, pulled my legs up, and rested my chin on my knees as I continued crying...

"Sounds like he's here..." he said as he left the room. I listened to the conversation going on as he came inside...

"Hey man – what's up?" Randall asked...

"I have a surprise for you..." Rashad answered...

"What'd you do now?" Randall asked as he perked up...

"I got you some pussy..."

"Again with this shit man? I already told you – I'm gonna wait until Clarisse is ready!" Randall laughed...

"My man..." Rashad said as he put his hand on Randall's shoulder... "She's ready..."

"What the fuck did you do?"

"Go on upstairs..." Rashad laughed. I heard him coming upstairs and I started to panic. When I heard Rashad following him I started praying...

"Oh God... please... no..." I whispered as I cried...

"What the fuck is this?!" Randall yelled when he opened the door and saw me naked, crying, and handcuffed to the bed...

"I told you – she ready..." Rashad smiled...

"Fuck you!" Randall yelled as he punched Rashad in the face and knocked him to the floor...

"I knew you were soft..." Rashad laughed as he wiped the blood from his mouth and stood up...

"What the fuck is wrong with you?! Why would you do this?!" Randall yelled...

"You'sa soft bitch-ass!" Rashad laughed...

"Did you rape her?"

"You been complaining about not getting' any pussy – there it is – you want it – take it!" I watched in horror as Randall took off his jacket and came over towards the bed...

"Please... please don't do this..." I begged...

"I'm not going to hurt you..." Randall said as he covered me with his jacket...

"Are you fuckin' serious? You don't want no pussy – you ain't never wanted no pussy – talkin' 'bout you gonna wait 'till she ready – ain't no way I'm spendin' money on a chick and she ain't givin' me no pussy – but I ain't no soft bitch-ass faggot like you.." I couldn't believe what happened next...

"I'll kill you!" Randall yelled as he rushed Rashad so fast they both lost their balance out the door... and down the stairs. I held my breath as I heard footsteps...

"Oh God... please don't let that be him..." I prayed as Randall came in the door...

"Did he rape you?" he asked as he sat down on the bed next to me and held me...

"Noo..." I cried...

"I'm calling the police..."

"Noo... please... they can't see me like this... please..." I cried...

"I'm sorry..." he said as he stood up, took his cell phone out of his pocket, and dialed 911...

"911 – What's your emergency?"

"He's dead..."

"He's dead?" I asked...

"Sir? Who's dead?"

"My best friend..."

"Did you kill him?"

"He raped my girlfriend..." he said as he hung up...

"He didn't rape me..." I whispered...

"Yes he did... understand?"

"Yes... I understand..." I answered as I shook my head to acknowledge I understood...

"You came over here to see me... he told you I'd be here soon... he attacked you... you tried to fight him off... he ripped your clothes off... he handcuffed you to the bed... I came in... I heard you screaming... I ran up here to help you... we fought... we fell down the stairs... and he broke his neck... understand?" I shook my head to acknowledge I understood...

Chapter 9

I knew I never had sex with Rashad so when the police asked me to do a rape kit, I refused. I argued that I was already mortified because they found me naked, handcuffed to the bed, and covered in bruises so instead of treating me like a suspect, they should allow me to have some dignity – and thank God, it worked. They never questioned Randall's statement because everything I went through basically corroborated everything he said.

Rashad's death was ruled an accident and Randall was the sole beneficiary on his insurance policy so he used that money to pay off his condo and pay for our honeymoon in Mystic, Connecticut. We got married in the judge's chambers at the court house and on our wedding night, I wasn't able to make love to him so Randall spent the night holding me and trying to comfort me.

When we got back from our honeymoon, I moved in with Randall and for the first two weeks, I'd wake up in the middle of the night shaking and crying, unable to go back to sleep. Whenever I went to take a shower, I'd hide my body from Randall if he came into the bathroom and it wasn't until he started taking showers in the guest bathroom that I was able to understand that he was hurting because he wanted to comfort me and I wouldn't let him so one day when I saw he was in the shower, I took off my robe, opened the shower door, stepped in, and broke down as he pulled me into his arms and held me. I looked up at him and saw that he had been crying right along with me and after being married for a month, we were making love in the shower. After we made love in the shower, Randall turned off the water, took me by the hand, led me out the shower, picked me up in his arms, carried me down the hall to the bedroom, and we made love in our bed as husband and wife for the first time.

I started going back to the gym and to my surprise, Randall had paperwork drawn up to have me named as partner and changed the name of the gym from R & R to C & R. We also hired another personal trainer – a woman named Kalli. Kalli was a breath of fresh air and she took over all of Rashad's clients' except Angela, who decided it was best for her to find another gym.

Tasha and Tisha gave us a chance and since they've started coming to the gym, they've invited their boyfriends to join, we've all grown closer, and our monthly happy hours continue to be lit!

Conversation with My Character, Rashad

"Hey..." Rashad greeted as I turned around...

"What the hell are you doing here?!"

"Calm down – I'm not here to hurt you... I just wanna talk..."

"I didn't invite you here!"

"If I waited for an invitation, I would've never been invited..."

"You're right..."

"Do you want me to leave?"

"No..."

"Thank you..." he said as he sat down..."

"Why are you here?"

"As I said... I wanna talk to you..."

"You don't wanna talk to me – you need to talk to me..."

"You should know... you created me..."

"Yes... I created you..."

"Why?"

"Why did I create you?"

"That's one question..."

"I needed to..."

"You needed to create a psychotic maniac?"

"Yes..."

"I'm not a psychotic maniac – you didn't have to do that to me!"

"You're not a psychotic maniac – you had a psychotic break – there's a difference..."

"You killed me!"

"I know – I'm sorry..."

"Are you?!"

"Yes..."

"Why'd you do it then?! All I did was get pussy – I never took it – you created me so you know that!"

"Yes – I created you – but I also put a face to the men that get away with it..."

"The men that get away with what?!"

"Men like you – you go from woman to woman to woman – you don't give a damn if she catches feelings or not – as far as you're concerned, she's nothing more than a conquest!"

"Now I get it..."

"Get what?"

"You created me... to get even..."

"No I didn't..."

"Yea right!" he laughed...

"I'm serious..."

"So you're telling me that it never happened to you?"

"Not me..."

"Someone else?"

"All my stories have an element of truth to them..."

"That doesn't answer my question..."

"It wasn't meant to..."

"Why'd you kill me?"

"I had to kill you..."

"You had to?! Why?!"

"Are you seriously asking me that after what you did to Clarisse?"

"You could've had me arrested! You could've had Randall bust me down to the white meat!"

"I could've written it that way – and Clarisse would've lost Randall – and you would've continued to be an arrogant, cocky, narcissistic mutha fucka that would've lost a friend – both of you would've lost a business – and instead of taking accountability for your actions, you would've blamed Randall for it all and moved on to your next conquest..."

"I never thought of it like that..."

"Clarisse didn't deserve that..."

"No she didn't..."

"Randall was a good man..."

"I know, I know!" he laughed...

"He deserved to be happy..."

"Yea... he did..."

"Are you still mad at me?"

"Naa... I get it..."

"Good..."

"Aiight – I won't keep you – I got things to do..." he said as he got up...

"You're dead!" I laughed...

"So is Helen..." he said as he smiled a sinister smile...

"Oh my God – are you serious?"

"You already know... you created me..." he laughed as he disappeared...

www.ingramcontent.com/pod-product-compliance
Lightning Source LLC
Chambersburg PA
CBHW070531130626
46555CB00003B/1370